45 p.

D1305056

Jody the mouse, is a magical toy. He was fashioned by The Wizard of Paint Creek. The Wizard is a skilled toy maker, who endows his toys with magical qualities - qualities only apparent to children with imagination.

Jody understands and speaks every language there is. He, and all the other mice that the Wizard made, know many wonderful things, which they share with those who believe in them.

Katie Murphy believed in Jody from the start. He became her family's guide on their trips through Michigan.

Jody's Michigan Adventure Books tell about all the things that happened to Jody, and Katie's other animal friends. You are invited to come along with the Murphy family. All you need to do is enter into Katie's imagination .

Great Places
Jody's Michigan Adventures
Michigan's Detroit

Summary: On one of their visits to Detroit, the
Murphys take along Jody, Katie Murphy's toy mouse,
and Gilbert, the egomaniacal toy frog. When Gilbert
sees an organ grinder's monkey in Greektown, he
remembers the awful time he had at the
Detroit Zoo. The Harambee apes hung him
from the highest bar in their cage
for being so arrogant

Written by Leigh A. Arrathoon & John J. Davio
Illustrated by Kenneth M. Hajdyla
Coloring by Mary Anne Strong

If you want more information on
Great Places, write for a free brochure
Paint Creek Press, Ltd.
P.O. Box 80547, Rochester, MI 48308-0001

ISBN 1-893047-02-4

Printed in China

Katie Murphy

Kevin Murphy

Mike Murphy

Mary Murphy

Jody

Gilbert

The Murphy family was eating in a Greek restaurant in Detroit. Of course, Jody the mouse and Gilbert the frog were there too. They are Katie Murphy's favorite toys. Katie is my little sister by the way. My name is Kevin.

"Sloo-oop! Sloooop!"

"Do you have to slurp your soup, Gilbert?" Jody shook his head.

"Indeed I do," declared Gilbert. "It tastes much better slurped. **Avgolemono.** (Pronounced ahv-go-lay-mo-no. Its a lemon and rice soup.) Absolutely extraordinary. Mmmm!"

Between loud, rude slurps, Gilbert talked about his family. He said he was part Greek. His Irish great grandmother had married a **Peloponnesian** bullfrog (a Greek from the mainland. Pronounced pello-po-nee-zhan). Even though he was a stuffed toy, Gilbert claimed his ancestors were real frogs.

Gilbert asked my sister Katie to buy him an **evzone** uniform (worn by riflemen in the Greek army). He put it right on. He looked just like a Greek soldier. He had a tassle on his hat.

Jody leaned over to hear what we humans across the table were saying. We were remembering all the things we had done that day.

"I liked the Eastern Market. That was cool!" said Katie.

"It was so early in the morning, I don't remember it," I complained.

"Oh, you missed the best part of the day." said Katie. "It was awesome. All the farmers were out selling their produce. The fruits and vegetables were as fresh as the morning air! But the best part was the people. Did you see that woman from Iran? She was wearing a **chador**."

"A what?" I asked.

"A **chador** - a veil. And there were Indian women in colorful **saris** (7 - 8 yards of cloth, wrapped around to form a skirt and a head or shoulder covering). It was like being in another world!" my sister said.

"There's a Middle Eastern Market across the bridge. What about that?! They had Arab bread and **dolma** (Turkish for stuffed grape leaves)," said my dad, Mike Murphy. "Now I liked that!"

"The best part of the day for me was breakfast," my dad continued. "When we went to Hamtramck and got those angel's wings, that was just what I needed."

"Michael!" said my mother, "Don't remind us that you had Polish pastry for breakfast. I'm just glad it was too early to get kielbasa, or you would have had some of that too."

"You bet!" dad said.

"What's kielbasa?" Katie asked.

"Mmmmm!" said dad.

"It's fattening! You don't need to know!" said our mother.

"Cool! What is it Dad?" I asked him.

"Well, it's like a hot dog," dad replied, "but you never tasted a hot dog like this! Man! Let's go get some!"

"Yeah!" I shouted.

"It's late," said our mother.

"Ah, but Mom! Anyway you promised we could go to Trapper's Alley," I reminded her.

"Well, I guess we can do that, but then we have to go home," she answered.

My dad paid the bill. Katie scooped Jody and Gilbert up. As we were crossing Monroe Street, we saw an organ grinder with a monkey!

"Oh, oh!" Gilbert whispered to Jody. "Do you remember what happened last year at the Detroit Zoo?" He was referring to last June. It wasn't just the zoo. Gilbert made everything we did painful.

That fateful June day, my mom took us kids to the town of Royal Oak. We got there early, so we had plenty of time to see everything on both big streets: Washington and Main.

There were cafés, restaurants, coffee shops, furniture, and clothing stores. But the best places were the **galleries** (places where artwork is displayed). There were beautiful glass and ceramic things in one place. In another place, we saw medieval knights and dragons.

We spent a long time looking at all the brightly colored things from South America in one of the galleries. Jody liked the hand-painted wooden animals. Katie bought a clay flower pot with three llamas sticking out of it.

When it came time to eat, we couldn't decide whether to have Lebanese, Thai, Mongolian, or Chinese food. Gilbert thought the Mongolian place would be nice because then he could put a little of everything in his bowl. He can be greedy sometimes! Of course he doesn't know anything about cooking. He didn't like the food he mixed together. Jody had to give him his bowl.

On a side street, there was a colorful kite shop. There were birds of prey, fish, warriors, animals, and whales. Katie and I each bought a kite.

You'd think Gilbert would have been satisfied after the trouble he got into at the zoo (which I will tell about in a minute). No. He even managed to get into mischief when we got home.

My sister says he stared at my big Samurai warrior kite. "You know," he said, clearing his throat, "My other grandfather Hughes used to be a famous flyer."

No one payed any attention to Gilbert until he went sailing past the windows. Jody rubbed his eyes. Sure enough, the little green pest was riding my Samurai kite!

"Haloo!" cried Gilbert, as he glided out of sight. He was wearing goggles and a flying ace scarf.

"I say! Gilbert! Are you sure you know what you're doing?!" Jody shouted, but it was too late. The beautiful Samurai kite had gone full circle. It smashed head on into the Maple tree.

Jody ran out to see if Gilbert was all right. He was under the tree, confused. The kite was smashed.

Well, at least this is what Katie tells me happened. All I know is, the person who destroyed my beautiful kite was selfish.

Anyway, during the day - before this "accident" with my kite - we went to the Royal Oak Zoo. That was another sorry misadventure.

Near the entrance to the zoo, is an **aviary** (a house where birds are kept). It's a tropical paradise, with very unusual birds and beautiful plants.

We visited the elephants, lions, and tigers. Then we watched the Great Apes of Harambee. Katie says Gilbert began to laugh loudly at one ape in particular. He even made faces at it.

"Stop that this instant!" Jody said to him, but Gilbert wouldn't listen. He had no idea what the ape was really like. He had no reason to make fun of it.

After a while the ape came as close to Gilbert and Jody as it could. It appeared to be jeering at Gilbert. It looked straight at him, pulled back its lips so all of its teeth were showing, and laughed.

"I don't see what it thinks is so funny," said Gilbert.

Katie, my mom, and I had gone off to eat hot dogs. Katie was tired. She had set Gilbert and Jody down very carefully. But then she forgot them. The ape spoke to the two abandoned toys. Imagine their surprise!

"My name's Macaba Macambo. You can call me Mac for short," the ape said to Jody.

"Hi Mac. My name's Jody Murphy." the mouse replied.

Gilbert's mouth hung open. The ape chewed his banana thoughtfully.

"Who's your green friend?" he asked finally.

"Uh, he lives at my house," Jody answered. He didn't want Mac to think that Gilbert was a friend.

"My name is Gilbert," said the frog, twirling his umbrella. (At this time, Gilbert was imitating his English ancestors. He was dressed in spats, and a straw hat. He was carrying an umbrella.)

"You look like an important fellow," remarked the ape, tossing his banana peel over his shoulder.

"I am! Sir Gilbert, at your service!"

The ape looked him up and down for a moment. He was obviously trying to understand the full meaning of Gilbert's words. Then he said, "Why don't you climb over here? I'll take you to our king."

"Oh, now, that's more like it! This is a fine fellow after all, this Mac. Knows he's dealing with an aristocrat. I'll be right there Mac, my good man! Coming Jody?"

Jody thanked Gilbert, but he thought he should be the one to stay behind to wait for Katie.

Well, from what the frog later told Katie, Mac took him into a large room, filled with apes. The largest ape was bigger and hairier than the rest. This big ape's lip curled with disgust when he saw Gilbert.

Mac addressed the king with respect. He spoke in a strange tongue. Gilbert guesses he said something like this:

"Your Highness. This green fellow is rude and very foolish. I think he needs to learn a lesson."

"What did you tell him, dear boy?" Gilbert asked. Mac smiled; the king frowned. Gilbert thinks the king's next words were:

"Hang him from the rafters. And leave him there."

Mac and one of his friends quickly surrounded the frog.

"I say. What are you going to do?" asked Gilbert in a frightened voice.

Without so much as a word, the apes grabbed the frog. They dangled him from a bar, high up in the monkey cage. They used his suspenders to hold him there. Then they took away his spats, his straw hat, and umbrella.

The king raced around from one bar to the next to get a good look at the green stranger. Gilbert thinks his next words were:

"He is strange looking. Truly, he's so odd, I have no desire to eat him." After that he spat, showing all of his great white teeth.

The frog was afraid for his life. And well he might have been. This king of the apes had a very poor opinion of him. In fact the apes appeared to be considering how best to torture the frog when Katie came looking for him.

"There he is!" Jody said. If he hadn't stayed behind, he would never have been able to lead Katie to Gilbert.

Gilbert was fortunate. A guard came. He climbed up and rescued that sorry frog.

"He's lucky," the guard said to Katie. "If he'd been in the Mandrill's house, he might have been eaten!"

The Mandrills live very near the great apes. They're bearded and maned, with blue faces and red noses.

Gilbert never forgot the way those Harambee apes had jeered at him. Jody wasn't surprised if, now, a year later, Gilbert felt afraid of the organ grinder's monkey in Greektown.

We crossed the street from the Greek restaurant where we had eaten. Trapper's Alley was in a big, tall building on the other side. It has Greek restaurants, junk food, and gift shops. The family explored all the floors.

The inside walls are brick. There are skylights in the ceiling, which is probably good for all the plants they have there. Gilbert and Jody slid down the banisters. My dad said that soon the alley would be a very exciting place, because they are going to have gambling casinos.

The family was supposed to go home. Then my dad saw an entrance to the Detroit People Mover right in Trapper's Alley.

"Let's just hop on it and go to the Ren Cen. What do you say, Mary?" (Mary is my mom.)

Mom was tired. She sighed. The rest of us ran toward the platform.

The little **monorail** (a train that runs on one rail instead of two) arrived in about two minutes. *Clickity clack, clickity clack*, it sang out, as it raced along its track.

Once inside the car, we sat in plastic seats facing the center. We got fantastic views of Detroit and the river. We talked about the Thunderfest - the world's largest hydroplane race. We had seen it on the Detroit River earlier in the day. Awesome!

Powerboats raced in the Detroit River. Their **rooster tails** (the water that shoots up in back of the boat) looked like showers of diamonds when the sunlight caught them.

"I want to come back next week for the Grand Prix," I said.

The Grand Prix is Indy-car racing. It's free to see the trials. Famous people come here to compete. You can watch it from Belle Isle.

I love Belle Isle. We went there in the spring. They have a wonderful white Italian marble fountain there. Its turtles, dolphins, lionesses, and Neptunes, all spray water.

The Belle Isle Conservatory is a huge greenhouse, full of unusual plants from around the world. Gilbert went wandering through the cactus plants. He thought he was in a Mexican desert.

Jody liked the fern room. It was so beautiful and warm. Each room was like being in another part of the world.

The Belle Isle Aquarium is the oldest aquarium in America. it was built in 1904. Gilbert and Jody stared at the giant **gourami** (a fish that hasn't changed in all the 25 million years its species has been on earth).

There are also electric eels, stingrays, anemones, and lots more!

Gilbert's favorite exibit had tiny frogs, all huddled together under a small log. It made him feel like the little guys' big brother. The tiny frogs looked afraid of the world outside.

There is also a zoo on Belle Isle. There are boardwalks above it so you can look down at the animals. There were **alpacas** (animals like the llama, from Peru), pink flamingoes, kangaroos, **emus** (nonflying Australian birds), **cassowaries** (tall birds from New Guinea), and **oryx** (large African and Asian antelope), to name a few. But Belle Isle is famous for its fallow deer. They range around the island.

We also got to go on the Belle Isle Slide. Gilbert and Jody shared a burlap mat. When they came to the first bump, Gilbert covered his eyes and screamed. When they got to the bottom, he said he would never do it again. That was all right with Jody.

The People Mover finally stopped at the Renaissance Center. We jumped out of the train. We went to the top of the 73-story Westin Hotel. There's a revolving restaurant there.

It was confusing Inside the Ren Cen. There were huge ficus trees everywhere. And there were oh so many pillars and ramps.

We took the elevator to the top of the Westin Hotel. We could see all of Detroit go by as the restaurant turned slowly around.

Gilbert got dizzy. Even though the restaurant was moving at a snail's pace, it was going too fast for him. Katie had to take him outside until his stomach settled.

The sun was setting. The whole city was bathed in red and gold rays. My dad and I talked about Detroit, and how it came to be the way it is today.

"You can't build a big city like this without money," Dad said gravely. "The money to build Detroit came from the car. Henry Ford didn't invent the first car. But he made a practical one that everyone could afford to buy. Then he found out how to mass produce it. When he produced many cars quickly, Henry saved alot of money. Because of this he could sell his product very cheaply."

"There were other important people in the auto industry besides Henry Ford," My dad continued. "The seven Fisher Brothers developed the 'closed auto body,' which they sold to General Motors. Before the Fishers came along, auto bodies were designed like horse-driven carriages. They were often open and always uncomfortable.

The rich Fishers built the elaborate Fisher building." We could see it from the top of the Westin.

"One of the seven brothers, Lawrence Fisher, was the head of Cadillac Motors," My dad went on.

"Lawrence was a big guy, who loved parties. In the 1920s, he built the Spanish-style Fisher Mansion. The place is a small copy of William Randolph Hearst's huge mansion in San Simeon, California. Fisher and Hearst (a famous newpaper publisher) were good friends."

"Another mansion in Rochester, Michigan, belonged to an auto **baron** (a man of great power). It was built by the widow of John Dodge, between 1926-29. John, and his brother Horace, worked as mechanics. Along with Ford, the Fishers, and Cadillac, the Dodges helped to make Detroit into Motor City. Christmas is a good time to visit Meadow Brook Hall. The house is richly decorated then.

Henry Ford's 1600-acre Fair Lane Estate is also open to the public. It was to have been designed by Frank Lloyd Wright, the famous architect. Ford had to change architects. The finished house is a mixture of modern and old styles.

If you visit Fair Lane you can see the room where Henry's good friend, Thomas Edison, stayed. You'll also see the station wagon Henry used when he and his friends went on their famous camping trips.

Kevin, maybe you'd like to visit the Ford Rouge Complex, or group of factories. Henry made everything he needed - finished steel, plastic, rubber, and glass - in this one place. By the 1920s, 10,000 cars a day were made here."

"The famous 'battle of the overpass' took place near the Rouge Complex. Henry Ford refused to listen to the new union of Walter Reuther. Instead he sent rough men to deal with the union men.

Unlike the earlier generations of auto barons, Henry's son Edsel, and his wife Eleanor, built a mansion that overlooks Lake St. Clair.

This house was completed in 1929. It is made like an ancient manor from the **Cotswold** region (a place in England). A small copy of the mansion was built as a playhouse for Josephine, Edsel and Eleanor's daughter.

You can see the study where Edsel Ford often wept. He was a brilliant designer. Henry Ford made Edsel president of the Ford Motor Company. But Henry wouldn't listen to his son's suggestions for changes. Once Henry destroyed a beautiful car Edsel had designed. He did this with a hatchet, in public!"

"Even though Henry Ford could be an awful person sometimes, he contributed a great deal to Detroit and to the country. One of the many good things he did was to spend his idle time building The Edison Institute, now known as The Henry Ford Museum and Greenfield Village."

"Oh, I remember the Village!" Katie interrupted. "I loved it there! When can we go again?"

"Yeah," I said, "I loved the Edison laboratory! I wouldn't mind having all those bottles of chemicals myself!"

"I liked the Firestone Farm. It was the Ohio boyhood home of Henry Ford's friend Harvey Firestone, the tiremaker. The farm raises and sells Merino sheep. They also have **Percherons** (draft horses), Poland China pigs, and Durham short-horned cows. I'd like to go back during Spring Farm Days," said Katie.

"I suppose you like that New England Farm from the 1780s (the one they call the Daggett Farm), the Suwanee Riverboat, the nineteenth-century Eagle Tavern, and - let me guess - the Cotswold Cottage," I mocked.

"Of course I like those places. What's wrong with that?!" Katie cried.

"Oh nothing," I sighed. "It's just that the purpose of the Henry Ford Museum and Greenfield Village is to show the progress of American civilization from farm to industry. The most important things to see are Henry Ford's factories and cars, Thomas Edison's labs, and the Wright Brother's bicycle shop. You're supposed to look at the buildings in the village - how and where the people lived. Then you go to the museum to see what they invented, and how it changed America."

"Boring!" Katie cried.

"I can't help it. That's the way it is." I was angry. Katie was just being herself.

"Pooh! I liked the Waterford General Store better than any of those places you mentioned," she said.

"It figures." I shook my head.

"Well, it just goes to show," said my father. "There's something for everybody at Henry's museum and village. Even though Henry Ford had some serious faults, he made many valuable contributions to this country."

No one said anything for a while. I think we didn't know whether there was a lesson in this for us or not.

"Hmph!" exclaimed Gilbert at last. "I wanted to see Motown - the house that made Michael Jackson, Diana Ross and the Supremes, Stevie Wonder, the Temptations, and many others famous. Now why didn't we go there? I could have worn my Elvis Presley outfit - the one with the tight pants!"

Now imagine a frog, with those skinny legs, dressed up to look like Elvis! Jody was horrified.

"Did you know Berry Gordy, Jr., the guy who started Motown, used to be an auto worker?" Jody asked him.

Gilbert couldn't think of anything to answer.

"You know what we didn't see?" said Katie? "We never went to Mexican Town. I'd like to see their market one of these days."

"Do you ever think about anything besides shopping?" I asked. "What about Dearborn, where they have all that delicious Lebanese food? They have Palestinians, Chaldean Iraquis, and Yemenese there too. What about The Detroit Institute of the Arts, or the Cranbrook Science museum? Those are pretty neat."

"What do you think buying Lebanese food is? It's shopping! And the Cranbook Science museum is boring! But, Christ Church is such a beautiful cathedral. It's especially fun to go there at Christmas time. It makes me feel like a medieval person when we sit in the monks' stalls on the side of the Church." said Katie.

"That is a beautiful Episcopal church," said our mother. "And Cranbrook school is famous for its artists. Remember St. Dunstan? He's the patron saint of the arts. His chapel is beneath Christ Church."

"Jody! JODY!" Gilbert screamed. The little green pain-in-the-we-won't-say-what had tumbled into a punch bowl that had been left on the bar.

"What are you doing in there?" asked Jody.

The frog made monstruous faces. He clawed at the sides of the bowl trying to get out. I saw him and lifted him onto the table. Was the frog grateful? No.

"Well. It's about time!" he hissed.

My dad paid the bill.

When we got home, Katie told me her version of our trip. Because she paid me, I typed her part of the story almost exactly the way she told it to me.